For His Name's Sake
... A Second Time Around

An Inspirational Book

by

Mary L. Henry-Watson

Copyright © 2003 by Mary L. Henry-Watson

For His Name's Sake
by Mary L. Henry-Watson

Printed in the United States of America

Library of Congress Control Number: 2003092116
ISBN 1-591605-97-0

All rights reserved. No part of this publication may be reproduced or transmitted in any form or by any means without written permission of the publisher.

Unless otherwise indicated, Bible quotations are taken from the King James Version of the Thompson Chain-Reference Bible. Fourth Improved Edition. Copyright © 1964, By B. B. Kirkbridge Bible Co., Inc.

Xulon Press
www.XulonPress.com

Xulon Press books are available in bookstores everywhere, and on the Web at www.XulonPress.com.

Contents

Dedication vii

Acknowledgments ix

Foreword xi

Preface xv

Chapters:
1. Obey, Turn It Over to God, and Try Again 19
   God of a second chance
2. Never Say Never Before You Say Yes 29
   A lesson learned
3. Beyond the Gap...37
   An unconditional love
4. Even the Bad Is For Our Good................................45
   Understanding the will of God
5. Time Produces Evidence of Spiritual Blessings 55
   Going from grace to grace
6. God's Glory Is Revealed in Every Situation..........69
   Survival through adversities
7. The End of Life Is Just a Puff Away 77
   Do whatever you can, while you can

Appendix 91
Unforgettable moments (A random survey)

Reflections 99

Epilogue 107

Dedication

This book is dedicated to God, our Redeemer; my Lord and Savior Jesus Christ; and the Holy Spirit, who revealed the titles of the seven chapters that are being shared with you, the reader.

It is my prayer that this book will be used as an instrument of blessings "For His Name's Sake," in order that God might be glorified.

Acknowledgments

To my first granddaughter, Ja'nel Davis, who is a great blessing to me, her grandfather, and the rest of the family. You were a powerful influence in my writing this book. You were the catalyst that was used by God to ignite the flame again. Thank you for being who you are in Christ.

To Tyla, Tierra, and Kendall, Grandma loves you, too. I pray that in years to come you will be inspired by this book, to have confessed Christ, and to have a personal and dedicated walk with him all the days of your lives.

To my wonderful children, Michael and Malandria, I thank God for you. Thanks for being the joy of our lives.

To my husband, for your love and patience, and to all grandmothers who contributed to the "Unforgettable Moments," a most appreciative thanks.

Foreword

Leaving the shelter and comfort of my parents' home when I graduated from college at the age of twenty-one to accept a teaching position at a high school/junior college in Mississippi was my first eye-opening experience.

Little did I know about the real world. However, I thank God for my parents who raised me in a Christian environment, and my accepting the Lord into my heart before the age of twelve.

Even though I was trained in the way I should go, this was a dangerous time for me. I had no worldly experience and no street smarts, and was very naïve and vulnerable. And, sometimes when we are removed from the influence of our home and church, we tend to go our own way.

During my first year of teaching and adjusting, I was befriended by a pastor's wife and at the same time was exploited by her husband, who was very prominent in the city. In addition, I was exploited by the principal who gave me the position I had for the first five years.

Sexual harassment was forbidden by Title VII of the Civil Rights Acts; however, most people were not aware of it and the laws had not been tested.

As a result of those unwanted, unwelcome experiences,

some things were said and done that I became ashamed of later, so I was tortured from the inside. When we repent and turn back to God, we can experience once again his presence and power in our lives. My God will remove the shame of sin, lift the burden of guilt, and renew hope within your heart.

After five years, and as the Holy Spirit would have it, I accepted a position in the nearby state of Alabama.

Being the first black teacher at this school that only a handful of black students were attending was a very traumatic experience for me. The name calling by the students and the staring and shunning by most of the teachers were hurtful and almost unbearable. This was a period in history when we were struggling for racial equality through demonstrations throughout the United States. Even though some civil rights laws had been passed, the KKK was still active and in control.

Little did I realize, at that time, that this was all part of a divine plan. God's hand was at work weaving the canvas, and I did not recognize it.

After that sixth year away from home, that season of my life was over and I ended up in the place I now call home. This was a place where some people thought that God did not exist, but according to the Word of God, where sin abounds, grace abounds much more. God is everywhere. His eyes are in every place, beholding the evil as well as the good.

Staying there was not a part of my plan. It was my intention to come to Las Vegas just for some rest and relaxation. I really wasn't sure of what I wanted to do next because of life's uncertainties.

As youngsters, when we leave home for one reason or another, we represent our parents. As Christians, we also represent a name that is above every name, and that name is **Jesus Christ.**

Foreword

Just as parents want their children to conduct themselves in a certain way to not bring shame and disgrace upon the family, our heavenly Father expects us to behave in a certain way to bring honor and glory to **his name.**

No matter who we are, we are still God's children, and we are required to establish and maintain a divine relationship with him. *"How great is the love the Father has lavished on us, that we should be called children of God"* (1 John 3:1 NIV). As children of God, he wants us to come to him by faith, believing that he knows, sees, and cares about every area of our lives, and that he will do something about it.

For he has assured us through his Word that he is faithful toward us. Sometimes young people feel that the only way they can "fit in" is by conforming to the ways of the world. Not so. We must choose to live by God's standards even if we are looked down upon, passed over for a promotion, or rejected by people thought to be friends. When God is for you, he is more than the world against you.

As an encouragement to those who are in the midst of a trying situation or temptation, the Bible teaches us: *"There hath no temptation taken you but such is common to man: but God is faithful, who will not suffer you to be tempted above that ye are able; but will with the temptation also make a way to escape, that ye may be able to bear it"* (1 Corinthians 10:13).

Preface

Many years ago, I had a desire to write a book about my first six years away from home. I started a manuscript when I moved to Las Vegas, but some how it got misplaced. I now believe that the Lord was saying, *"It is not yet time to write."*

After leaving the teaching profession, I began a new career working for a company that was a prime contractor for the government at the Nevada Test Site in Mercury, Nevada, which was approximately sixty-five miles from Las Vegas.

I received training and attended various workshops and seminars throughout the United States in preparation for my new career. As a result, I wanted to write about my experiences in traveling, the challenges I faced as a woman with the type of job I had, and the financial rewards I received. Because of certain circumstances, I believe the Lord was saying once again, *"It is not yet time to write, for things will come to pass because of God's season."*

Those of you who love to cook know that, in a given recipe, if the finished product is to come out the way it was intended, you must use the right ingredients and follow the directions carefully. For example, you may need to preheat the oven to a certain temperature before baking a certain food.

For my writing to be what God wanted it to be, he had to turn on the heat first so that I would become spiritually ready to reflect more of the image of his Son, and that he might be glorified.

When I attempted to write on my own, I was still not at the right temperature; I was neither hot nor cold. I was a lukewarm Christian. When I became the right temperature, it became my time, for God has a great concern for the finished product. He is the author and finisher of our faith.

In the year 2001, the Lord honored my request to write and allowed me to go forward with great confidence based on the Scriptures from the thirty-sixth chapter of Ezekiel, where God was talking about renewing and restoring Israel for his holy name's sake. He wanted to remind me of my being forgiven and my spiritual transformation, which was similar to the process outlined below for Israel:

> *Therefore say unto the house of Israel, thus saith the Lord God; I do not this for your sakes, O house of Israel, but for mine holy name's sake, which ye have profaned among the heathen, whither ye went. And I will sanctify my great name, which was profaned among the heathen, which ye have profaned in the midst of them; and the heathen shall know that I am the Lord, saith the Lord God, when I shall be sanctified in you before their eyes. For I will take you from among the heathen, and gather you out of all countries, and will bring you into your own land. Then will I sprinkle clean water upon you, and ye shall be clean: from all your filthiness, and from all your idols, will I cleanse you. A new*

Preface

> *heart also will I give you, and a new spirit will I put within you: and I will take away the stony heart out of your flesh, and I will give you an heart of flesh. And I will put my spirit within you, and cause you to walk in my statutes, and ye shall keep my judgments, and do them.* (Ezekiel 36:22–27)

Now, as I accomplish this burning desire, I will share with you how through faith and obedience, the power of the Holy Spirit moved in my life. I will also share how I was given a second chance and was taken from grace to grace because of his unconditional love.

I truly thank God for the unmerited favors he has shown toward me. He is truly the God of a second chance, many times over.

There is a reality in the Scripture from Romans 8:28: *"And we know that all things work together for good to them that love God, to them who are the called according to his purpose."*

I trust that this book will inspire you to look at life through the eyes of Christ. May he continue to bless you as you start and or continue on this spiritual journey. According to God's Word, we can delight ourselves in him, and he will give us the desires of our hearts.

CHAPTER 1

Obey, Turn It Over to God, and Try Again

*Enter ye in at the strait gate: for wide is the gate,
and broad is the way, that leadeth to destruction,
and many there be which go in thereat:
Because strait is the gate, and narrow is the way,
which leadeth unto life, and few there that find it.*
(Matthew 7:13–14)

A few years after I moved to Las Vegas, I was having several recurring dreams but I had no clue what they meant. I now realize that the dreams were visions from God, but I was too unskilled in the faith at that time to understand what they meant. As my relationship grew in the Lord, the Holy Spirit brought the dreams back to my remembrance with meaning.

I recall one in particular. I was on my way somewhere, and for me to get there, I had to drive across a one-way, narrow bridge, with water as far as I could see on both sides. There was no end in sight.

When I would get to the beginning of the bridge, the

fear of driving off the bridge and drowning would come over me. It was so narrow that it looked impossible for me to drive through to the other side.

When I tried to find an alternate route to where I was headed, I could not find one, and became very frustrated, and soon I would awaken from this dream.

In the book of Daniel, I read where he miraculously interpreted King Nebuchadnezzar's first dream as a vision from God. But, I did not seek an interpretation, for it was the Holy Spirit who pricked my heart to let me know that I had to surrender all.

In retrospect, Jesus was saying to me, *"I am the way, the truth, and the life: no man cometh unto the Father, but by me"* (John 14:6).

We have two different *lifestyles* to choose from:

1. Popular—worldly pleasures, self indulgence
2. Unpopular—self denial, depending on God

God is merciful, faithful, and long suffering toward us. He does not want any of us to perish. Ultimately, we have to make that choice. Jesus said in Matthew 6:24: *"No man can serve two masters: for either he will hate one, and love the other; or else he will hold to the one, and despise the other. Ye cannot serve God and mammon."* If you were to take the test of self-denial, would you pass it?

Jesus said in Matthew 16:24: *"If any man would come after me, let him deny himself, and take up his cross, and follow me."* There were two disciples recorded in the book of Matthew who failed the test. Demas also failed the test in the fourth chapter of 2 Timothy.

Sometimes self-denial may mean leaving a good paying job: *"And after these things he went forth, and saw a publican, named Levi, sitting at the receipt of custom: and he said unto him, Follow me"* (Luke 5:27).

Our lives can be overwhelmed with things we are doing that do not build the kingdom. As a result, we can become frustrated, discontented, and burned out.

Self-sacrificing for Christ's sake is profitable. When we do this, he will pay us many times over in this world and give us eternal life in the world to come.

God of a Second Chance

Spending so much time away from home daily did not allow time for me to adequately study the Word of God and fulfill the responsibilities I had taken on in the church. A serious choice had to be made.

After being led by the Holy Spirit, I made the decision to leave my out-of-town, lucrative position.

Approximately eight months later, the Holy Spirit revealed to me that I would be offered a position and the amount per hour, which was a lesser consideration, by the same company, in the Las Vegas area. Being led by the Holy Spirit, I accepted the position. I was not surprised with the offer because it had been revealed to me.

This second time around with the company gave me more time to study and meditate on the Word of God. God will provide a window of opportunity to prepare you for the ministry he has ordained for you.

As young parents, you can easily get caught up in the world's system of getting ahead. You can spend countless hours and immeasurable energy trying to impress, get a promotion, bigger house, larger boat, etc., instead of seeking God first. *"But seek ye first the kingdom of God, and his righteousness; and all these things shall be added unto you"* (Matthew 6:33). *"For what is a man profited, if he shall gain the whole world, and lose his own soul? or what shall a man give in exchange for his soul?"* (Matthew 16:26).

In this life we must make a choice of whether it is going to be:

- Heaven or hell
- Good or evil
- Right or wrong
- Saint or sinner
- Security or insecurity
- Salvation or condemnation

There is no in between. As Christians, we are not to live half-hearted, double-minded lives before God. We must walk according to his righteousness.

Jesus is saying to the half-hearted in Revelation 3:15–16: *"I know thy works, that thou art neither cold nor hot: I would thou wert cold or hot. So then because thou art lukewarm, and neither cold nor hot, I will spue thee out of my mouth."*

Walking with God includes the elements of **faith and obedience,** and it is proven by the paths we take. He is a loving Father who cares about all of his children. If we truly love him (John 14:15), we will keep his commandments to stay on the straight and narrow path.

When we are out of the will of God, our blessings are delayed and we cause a lot of drama that goes on in our lives: setbacks, disappointments, heartaches, and sometimes pain.

When Jonah was not obedient and failed God the first time, God did not give him up. The most encouraging words that we who have failed God can hear are from Jonah 3:1: *"And the word of the Lord came unto Jonah the second time."*

Have you ever thought of this question: "If Jonah had refused to go to Nineveh the second time, would God have destroyed the city?" If we continually refuse to obey God, he will raise up another instrument, for God's will must be done.

God is truly a restorer and the God of the second chance.

Obey, Turn It Over to God, and Try Again

1 Peter 2:9–10 tells us: *"But ye are a chosen generation, a royal priesthood, an holy nation, a peculiar people; that ye should shew forth the praises of him who hath called you out of darkness into his marvellous light; Which in time past were not a people, but are now the people of God: which had not obtained mercy, but now have obtained mercy."*

When things get locked up in our lives, it will take certain keys to open them. The first key is Jesus, who will restore you to wholeness. He restores the body, mind, and soul. He is the same yesterday, today, and forevermore. Reference Scriptures:

> *He restoreth my soul: he leadeth me in the paths of righteousness for his name's sake.* (Psalm 23:3)

> *Restore unto me the joy of thy salvation; and uphold me with thy free spirit.* (Psalm 51:12)

> *For I will restore health unto thee, and I will heal thee of thy wounds, saith the Lord; because they called thee an Outcast, saying, This is Zion, whom no man seeketh after.* (Jeremiah 30:17)

We must participate in the restoration process through the next two keys. Key number two is repentance. Reference Scriptures:

> *The Lord is not slack concerning his promise, as some men count slackness; but is longsuffering to us-ward, not willing that any should perish, but that all should come to repentance.* (2 Peter 3:9)

> *I say unto you, that likewise joy shall be in heaven over one sinner that repenteth, more than over ninety and nine just persons, which need no repentance.* (Luke 15:7)

> *If we confess our sins, he is faithful and just to forgive us our sins, and to cleanse us from all unrighteousness.* (1 John 1:9)

> *Have mercy upon me, O God, according to thy loving kindness: according unto the multitude of thy tender mercies blot out my transgressions.* (Psalm 51:1)

Finally, the third key is obedience. Obedience to the Lord has always been considered vital. It was disobedience that caused Adam and Eve to be cast out of the Garden of Eden, and it was disobedience that kept Moses from entering the Promised Land.

God spoke to Solomon in 2 Chronicles 7:14: "*If my people, which are called by my name, shall humble themselves, and pray, and seek my face, and turn from their wicked ways; then will I hear from heaven, and will forgive their sin, and will heal their land.*"

Other reference Scriptures:

> *And thou shalt return and obey the voice of the Lord, and do all his commandments which I command thee this day.*
> (Deuteronomy 30:8)

> *A blessing, if ye obey the commandments of the Lord your God, which I command you this day.* (Deuteronomy 11:27)

Obey, Turn It Over to God, and Try Again

> *But this thing commanded I them, saying, Obey my voice, and I will be your God, and ye shall be my people: and walk ye in all the ways that I have commanded you, that it may be well unto you.* (Jeremiah 7:23)

> *But the men marvelled, saying, What manner of man is this, that even the winds and the sea obey him!* (Matthew 8:27)

If we come to him with a contrite heart and confess our sins, he is faithful and will forgive us and cleanse us so we can start over again. Because we are just a vessel in his hands, he can put the broken pieces of our lives back together and make us whole again. When the broken pieces of our lives are put back together again, the Holy Spirit is back at work within us, ready to contain us. You may feel as though you are on a leash, because when the fleshly or earthly desires draw you away and you attempt to go in an opposite direction, you will feel a yank on the strap. Those desires are then pulled away, and you are back on the right path.

Questions for Personal Meditation

How do you think God feels about you if you made a mess of your life?

Has God ever given you a second chance?

Do you think that it was easy for God to forgive you? Why or why not?

Has there ever been a time when you doubted the presence of God? Was it because of some unconfessed sin?

Why do we find it easier sometimes to obey man rather than God?

Has denying of yourself ever been a problem for you?

Have you made the right choice for your life today, based on the will of God?

A Prayer from the Heart

Eternal God our Father, I am so grateful for the faithfulness you have shown toward us. You are truly the God of many chances. Thank you for allowing us to turn around and start over in the life you have ordained for us.
As we proceed on the spiritual journey, please continue to give us the spirit of obedience and faith.
Order our steps that we might walk therein.
We ask it all in the precious name of your Son, Jesus Christ, Amen.

CHAPTER 2

Never Say Never Before You Say Yes

*Trust in the Lord with all thine heart; and
lean not unto thine own understanding.
In all thy ways acknowledge him, and he
shall direct thy paths.*
(Proverbs 3:5–6)

When it comes down to making decisions on some things, we have all been guilty at one time or another of making them without consulting God. We have made some bad decisions in our lives. Some were crucial, and some were not so crucial. Nevertheless, God will never turn his back on us. He is always standing at the door of our hearts, knocking, sometimes releasing some pressure so that it might open for him to come in.

The Bible teaches us that before every man lies a wide, pleasant road that seems right, but it ends in death. I learned that the very thing that we say we will never do may already be in God's plan for our lives.

When I was in college it was normal for us to talk about

the kind of man we wanted to marry, setting the criteria based on the world's standards.

During one conversation, I remember saying that I never wanted to marry a military man or a preacher. Many others can identify with the statement I have just made.

I thought at the time that I had convincing reasons for my position. Well! I ended up with a package deal. God united me in marriage with a military man who later accepted his divine calling as a minister of the gospel.

On several occasions, during my acknowledgments, after accepting my calling into the ministry, I would recognize my husband for his support of my ministry and thank him in public. Then I would proceed to tell the story of a mentor I had in college by the name of Dr. Erna B. Jones, who was a graduate of Cornell University in Ithaca, New York.

She was a very inspiring professor who encouraged all her students to pursue the highest level of degree we could obtain. She was so convincing, I thought that the more degrees I held, the more options I would have and the better my chances of marrying a doctor or lawyer, and there would be a line to choose from. Not to my disappointment, though, I never saw that line. On one occasion, while I was speaking about this, one of the members came to me after the service and said that my husband had both hands at the top of his jacket as though he was saying, "Look what you got—you got me!" When I was speaking, I thought they were laughing at what I was saying, but apparently they were laughing at him making those gestures.

Even though I said "never" before I acknowledged God concerning my mate, and I did not get the doctor or lawyer who would help me become financially secure, which can be temporary, God gave me what I needed, for I realized that God knew what was best for me.

God gave me my husband, who was conferred the

Doctor of Divinity Degree from Brighter Day Theological Seminary of Las Vegas, Nevada, in conjunction with Trinity Hall College and Seminary in Colorado, in 1984. We now have lasting security that is not temporary but eternal in Christ. He has divine ownership of everything.

> *The earth is the Lord's, and the fulness thereof;*
> *the world, and they that dwell therein.*
> (Psalm 24:1)

A Lesson Learned

Saying yes to God's will allows you to establish a divine relationship with his Son, and keeps you from sudden destruction. Our benefits are secure in the Scripture found in Matthew 12:50. Jesus said, *"For whosoever shall do the will of my father which is in heaven, the same is my brother, and sister, and mother."* Jesus also said in Luke 8:21: *"my mother and my brethren are those which hear the Word of God, and do it."*

We who have accepted Christ as our personal Savior were bought with a price. It is no longer us, but Christ who lives in us. It is in him that we live and move and we are who we are.

The Scriptures tell us that God owns everything: the earth, the fullness thereof, the world, and they that dwell therein. As a result, we are just stewards or managers of whatever God has entrusted us with, and it is required of us that we be found trustworthy.

As a steward, giving to others was a privilege I enjoyed and still do. However, I had a problem with not acknowledging God as to whether or how I should spend my finances for personal pleasures. I felt that since I had labored, I did not need any guidance in what to do with it. I was wrong. I learned that when we fail to acknowledge God in *all* our ways and instead trust our own judgment, we will fail in our efforts.

We need the wisdom from God to direct us in the right path, especially in dealing with our mates, raising our children and grandchildren, spending money, and communicating effectively with others.

If you are having some difficulty now in asking God for help in making any decisions, I exhort you to trust God. When you trust God, he has promised that:

1. he will guide you into pleasant paths.
2. he will help you make the right decisions in anything you undertake.
3. he will guide you in the midst of uncertainties.
4. he will guide you unto the end of life.

I am reminded of a song, "I'll Trust you Lord," with words and music by Donnie McClurkin. In the musical composition, he hears Jesus singing the following lyrics:

> I know that faith is easy when every thing is going well.
> But, you can still believe in me when your life's a living hell.
> And when all things around you seem to quickly fade away,
> There's just one thing I really want to know.
>
> Will you let go?
> Will you stand on my word?
> Against all odds will you believe what I have said?
> What seems impossible

Never Say Never Before You Say Yes

Will you believe?
Every promise I made will you receive?

I know how bad it hurt you when that
 loved one's life came to an end.
And when they had to leave you, you
 said you'd never love again.
But will you trust that I can help you and
 I'll never turn away?
Will you trust me, child, no matter, come
 what may?

What if it hurts?
What if you cry, oh child?
What if it doesn't work out the first time
 that you try?
What if you call my name
And you don't feel me near?
Will you still believe in me or will you
 fear, my child?

The songwriter then encourages every believer to join with him by answering:

I will trust you, I will trust you, Lord.
No matter how hard the road might seem,
Every step I take, in my sadness, in all of
 my hurt,
Every day of my life I will trust you,
 because you never fail.

Questions for Personal Meditation

Is seeking God's will a major part of your life?

Why do you think it is important to acknowledge God?

Instead of seeking what you want, do you strive to do God's will?

Are you being disobedient to the will of God?

How do you feel about being obedient, even to some rules you don't like?

Has God put a vision and a passion in your heart to follow him?

Is he calling you to give up something so you will follow him faithfully?

A Prayer from the Heart

Our Father, knowing that you are the all-knowing, all-seeing, and all-caring God, grant us this day the wisdom to acknowledge you for direction and guidance in all the things we endeavor to undertake. We realize that the lessons we learn from being outside of your will are hard. Nevertheless, those trials and errors can build our faith and strengthen our character. Thank you for your grace and mercy. In Jesus' name we pray, Amen.

CHAPTER 3

Beyond the Gap

*And I sought for a man among them, that
should make up the hedge,
and stand in the gap before me for the land,
that I should not destroy it:
but I found none.*
(Ezekiel 22:30)

Are you willing to allow God to work in your life, in any way he chooses, so you will be a hedge of protection through righteousness for someone else?

Is there anyone like Moses, who stood before God in the breach to turn his wrath away from the children of Israel so they would not be destroyed?

In the Scripture, God was looking for someone who would take a stand against evil to keep the nation of Judah from being destroyed, and he found none.

Sin will destroy a nation just as it does individuals. When no one stands in the gap, evil pours in like water from a broken pipe.

God is still looking for men and women to participate in people's lives, giving assistance and support wherever needed.

We have heard throughout the ages that grandparents have always come up to the forefront and stood in the gap for their grandchildren. They opt to care for, provide for, and nurture them. They are also a positive influence while they develop a strong bond with them.

But in my case, being led by the Holy Spirit, I took on and acted out the role of a *new mother* during the formative years of my first granddaughter's life, going beyond what is normally expected.

Some did not understand why I went as far as I did, but the Lord knew: *"For my thoughts are not your thoughts, neither are your ways my ways, saith the Lord. For as the heavens are higher than the earth, so are my ways higher than your ways, and my thoughts than your thoughts"* (Isaiah 55:8–9).

I never gave much thought to being a grandmother. In fact, I had no grandmother mentors that I could emulate within my close family structure.

I never knew my maternal and paternal grandparents. I never had the opportunity for them to nurture me, to teach me how to bake old-fashioned cookies, to share stories with me of how my parents were as children, to call me and say, "I am praying for you," or just to spend some quality time with me. I believe that I missed a wonderful opportunity to get to know them and to learn from them. However, my mother was a loving and proud grandmother to our children during the first five and six years of their lives at a distance. They did get a chance to spend one summer with her in Louisiana before she went to be with the Lord.

Someone once said that becoming a grandparent will happen whether we want it to happen or not, whether we are ready for it or not. This is a role we do not choose, but for the most part graciously accept. Many years ago, grandmothers were perceived as being over-the-hill, semi-retired, or ready for a rocking chair. That image has changed. Today's grandmother is as young as thirty-five years of age, energetic, and very much into her career.

I believe now that the Lord bestowed upon me one of the most valuable gifts I could ever receive. This beautiful gift, this wonderful favor, was in the good, acceptable, and perfect will of God, and for this I am grateful.

It all started when I got a call from our daughter who was attending college in the southern part of the country.

We were devastated. When things go wrong in our lives, three questions come to mind: Why me? Why this? And why now? A lot of other questions immediately came to my mind: Where did we go wrong? Why did she do this? What are we going to do? What about her education? What will the people in the church say or think? It was as though we had been betrayed.

It was only during the calm that the still, firm voice of God gave me the assurance and guidance that I needed in what we were to do.

I am thankful for the third person of the Godhead (the Holy Spirit) who waits to take control of our lives to indwell, empower, encourage, counsel, teach, guide, and remind us.

The Holy Spirit brought back to my remembrance when our daughter had gone away to college and the next year our son entered the military to pursue his career in special forces. I walked the hallway many nights during that time. I would look into their rooms, crying and praying to the Lord about my loneliness and how I missed them. Frequent calls, and even letters, did not take the place of them being at home.

Usually in life, when it comes to the empty-nest stage, spouses would say to each other, "We can really enjoy ourselves now."

This was not the case for me. A strong bond existed

between the children and me. I felt as though a plug out of my heart was missing and the hole needed to be mended or replaced. I did not want to let go of the very things I held so dear. We need to let go and trust God and stand on his Word because of his unconditional love.

I had a loving husband who was a good provider, but he was preoccupied in his work and ministry. I was not included in them most of the time.

But, when we submit ourselves to God, he hears our cries because we are his people. He knows what's best for us and will work things out for our good.

I really felt unique in assuming my role as a grandmother after accepting the full responsibility of allowing our daughter to continue her education in the state where she was attending college. In the days that followed, God proved himself to me, time and time again, and I am sure that I was not alone.

I read an article in the *AARP Bulletin* entitled "The States" where it said that grandparents are on the rise as caregivers. Since 1990 there's been nearly a thirty-percent increase in the number of children being raised by grandparents. Census 2000 data show more than 4.5 million children living in 2.4 million grandparent-headed households. It also stated that many of the grandparents were divorced or widowed. There was a great generation gap when it came to homework. With old math and new math and with the new technology, some grandparents felt that they could not help them with it. It also pointed out that help of all kinds is available.

Becoming a grandmother caused me to flourish and the relationship with my husband to get back on track. Raising our granddaughter became a *"we thing"* instead of a *"me thing."* Together we began to focus more on God and on the things we were required to do according to the Word of God.

Through this opportunity, God gave me another chance to do more of some things I did not have time to do with my children when I worked sixty-five miles from home, leaving home at 5:00 A.M. and returning around 6:00 P.M.

Over a period of time, it can take a toll on your mind, body, and spirit.

By this time I was working normal hours in town, so I had ample time to:

- Read to and pray with her each night and in the mornings before school. I did not have to pray on the run. Prayer had become a priority.

- Attend parent-teacher conferences.

- Attend after-school activities she was involved in.

In addition, after taking the company buy-out, I was able to retire early. This afforded me the opportunity to sit in my granddaughter's classroom as a volunteer to observe and help some of the other students with their reading and spelling.

Going beyond the gap also afforded me the opportunity to make right some wrongs, and to be there when she was hurting, not only to listen and be sympathetic, but also to give some spiritual advice.

An Unconditional Love

Jesus made it right for the wrong that was started in the Garden of Eden because sin had entered in and separated us from God: *"But your iniquities have separated between you and your God, and your sins have hid his face from you, that he will not hear"* (Isaiah 59:2).

First, Jesus stood in the gap and bridged it by reconciling sinful man back to his Father, so we can have that wonderful relationship and fellowship again and eternal life. *"And all things are of God, who hath reconciled us to himself by Jesus Christ, and has given us the ministry of reconciliation"* (2 Corinthians 5:18).

I believe he also went beyond the gap as our great high priest who has gone into the heavens and is sitting on the right hand of God interceding for us. His atoning blood is still purging our conscience from dead works so we can serve the living God.

Questions for Personal Meditation

What are some things you find most difficult about standing in the gap for others?

Have you ever gone beyond what was required of you and felt good about doing it?

Have you ever felt that others did not deserve the things that you could do for them?

What are your thoughts on loving the unlovable unconditionally?

What have you yield to God and trusted him in faith to work it out for you?

Do you think that God is pleased with the way you serve him?

Do you think that the role you are now playing in the lives of grandchildren can be improved?

Prayer from the Heart

Thank you, Father, for giving me the opportunity to go beyond the gap and how you demonstrated your unconditional love for me during those difficult times of uncertainties. Thank you for the great privilege of grand parenting. Touch the lives of all grandparents and help them understand the importance of obedience to you. Help them to appreciate whatever role you have allowed them to play in the lives of their grandchildren, and to accept it with great joy, realizing that you will never leave them nor forsake them. For it is in the precious name of your Son, Jesus, that we pray, Amen.

CHAPTER 4

Even the Bad Is For Our Good

*And we know that all things work together
for good to them that love God,
to them who are the called according
to his purpose.*
(Romans 8:28)

It is not easy to comprehend the fact that some bad or unpleasant things that happen to us may actually be for our good, and it is difficult to understand the will of God apart from his Word. In the book of Psalms, he reminds us that he will withhold no good thing from us if we walk uprightly. So, the good thing can be the bad thing that happened for a moment.

Here is an excerpt from the book entitled *Joseph—God's Man in Egypt* by Leslie B. Flynn: "The story of Joseph has been called the Old Testament Romans 8:28. Cruelty, slander, ingratitude—these tangled, dark threads were woven by a sovereign Artist into a beautiful, bright pattern. With God, there is no accident or chance. Man proposes; God disposes.

Though others may treat us nastily, God is still on the throne, directing human affairs, able to use dirty deeds against us to effect his perfect will."

God had chosen Joseph for leadership, and God had to prepare him for the great task. God has chosen and will choose many others for leadership to affect his kingdom, and at any time in our lives any one of us may be God's man or woman in Egypt. But, rest assured that God will bring you out victoriously.

God does not want us to wallow in the disappointments of life. When bad things happen in our lives, he wants us to look beyond the situations and be at peace, and live with faith and courage. The Holy Spirit reminds us that through our disappointments, we can hold on to the truth that he will never leave us nor forsake us. We should say, "God, I know you are working the situation out for my good."

In the life of Fanny Crosby, a composer of thousands of songs, we have seen the power of God worked for the good, for truly she was more than a conqueror. Some time ago, I read that when she was only a few weeks old, an erroneous treatment of an eye infection caused her to become blind. Instead of weeping and feeling sorry for herself, she dedicated her blindness to God, to be used for his glory.

Out of her deep Christian experience, she composed numerous gospel hymns. In her very familiar testimonial song "Blessed Assurance," it appears that she seemed to have forgotten that she was blind with phrases such as "watching and waiting" and "looking above." Even though she was physically blind, I believe she was seeing with a spiritual eye, because she was secure in Christ. Many of us seek God for what we can see and get with the natural, rather than what we can become in the spiritual.

God has made himself and his will known to us through his Word. We are required to study the Word of God and hold this knowledge with "all spiritual wisdom and understanding." We must be able to apply what is known to us from the Scriptures in our daily lives. Knowing the will of God is not enough. It is putting what we know into practice that counts so we will live a life worthy of God.

Jesus is our perfect example of the New Testament Romans 8:28. Jesus came to do the will of his Father, to seek and to save those who were lost. As a result, he was rejected by his own, tempted by Satan, hated without a cause, smitten and spat upon, pierced in his hands and feet, mocked and insulted, given gall and vinegar, pierced in his side, betrayed by Judas, deserted by Peter, subjected to an illegal trial, and finally crucified with sinners. All these horrible things that happened to him were for our good.

It was not until I went through some personal trials in my home, on the job, and yes, in the church, which helped me to develop my Christian character and faith, that I was awakened to the reality of the above Scripture in Romans 8:28. God's divine purposes are unfailing. We can claim the promises in this verse because of verses 29 and 30, which state: *"For whom he did foreknow, he also did predestinate to be conformed to the image of his Son, that he might be the firstborn among many brethren. Moreover whom he did predestinate, them he also called: and whom he called, them he also justified: and whom he justified, them he also glorified."*

I am convinced that God saved me and called me with a holy calling, not according to my own works, but according to his own purpose and grace, which was given me in Christ before the world began.

When things seem to go crazy in our lives, we sometimes lose sight of God's love, his presence, and the hope that he will work things out for us. We must never allow the enemy to sow seeds of doubt or confusion in our hearts because God has a predetermined plan for each of us, and he will work it out.

Have you ever used your children or someone or something else as a crutch to help you through life, and when that crutch was removed, you felt lonely, helpless, and deserted, you thought your world was falling apart, and you wondered how you were going to continue? When this happens, we have a tendency to forget that Christ came that we might have life with him.

The realization is that when your life takes a sudden change, by submitting to the will of God, he can and will use your grandchild to ignite your flame again, and you can continue on this journey walking upright with faith, courage, wisdom, and grace.

God's Predetermined Plan at Work

One of my granddaughter's teachers was supposed to have completed and mailed an application to a local cultural center so my granddaughter could compete in a talent competition. For some unknown reason, the application was not mailed in a timely manner. Naturally, she was very disappointed because this would have been her first time competing in a pageant.

I assured her that this was not her time, and that God had something better for her. She was also reminded that God does answer our prayers; sometimes yes, sometimes no, and sometimes wait. This was her waiting period. This was God's intent beforehand.

A few months later, we received in the mail a letter and application indicating that she had been recommended to participate in a scholarship and recognition program, to be held at one the local hotels. You can imagine how excited and thankful she was after she read the letter. We had about one month to prepare for the talent and interview competition.

Just being a part of this program was a blessing and great joy. Actually winning top honors was not our foremost thought. We were just thankful to God that she was selected to participate and that she completed all the requirements before the deadline.

As God would have it, Ja'nel was crowned Miss Pre-Teen Nevada Junior for the year 1997–1998. God's divine plan is unfailing.

From this experience, I believe her faith in God began to increase. God will allow things to happen in our lives to make us aware that in every situation, he is in control.

Ephesians 3:20, paraphrased from the Living Bible, says, *"Glory be to God who by his mighty power at work within us is able to do more than we would ever dare to ask or even dream of—infinitely beyond our highest prayers, desires, thoughts, or hopes."* This verse declares that God works in us! God works through us! And God is glorified in us! These things are true because we are joint heirs with Christ, his son. When bad things happen, there is no need to stay down in the dumps. He will give us the ability to handle hardship over a long haul and to press on against insurmountable odds with relentless determination.

Understanding the Will of God

Understanding the will or desire of God includes knowing who God is and our purpose in life. God has made himself and his will known to us in his Word. God's will is sovereign and can be known. We can prove that it is God's will and that it can and will be done.

In our relationship with God, we can see his will in:

- **Our calling:** Just as Paul was called to be an apostle of Jesus Christ, through the will of God, we can have a divine calling in various ministries for his purpose. We were predestined, called, justified, and glorified. Thanks be unto God.

- **Our prayer lives:** If we ask anything according to his will, he will hear us, and we can have the things we desire of him. For we pray that his will be done on earth as it is done in heaven.

- **Our whole lives:** We don't have to live the rest of our lifetime in the flesh to the lust of men, but according to the will of God. It is his desire that none will perish.

- **Our instructions:** We can ask him to teach us his will and accept it because he is our God, and like a loving father, he will lead us into righteousness. He is the way, the truth, and the life (John 14:6).

- **Our daily work:** We are created to do good works, and as servants of Christ we are to do his will with all our hearts so we will receive his praise instead of the praise of men.

- **Our plans:** We do not know what is going to happen when we make our plans from day to day, week to week, month to month, or year to year. I do know that if it is God's will, our plans will come to fruition, and we can boast in him and not in ourselves.

- **Our travels:** We don't have to be dismayed when we hear or read about tragedies occurring by different modes of transportation, especially air travel for whatever reason. We can be safe and have prosperous journeys by the will of God.

- **Our suffering:** It is better to suffer for doing good than for doing evil. We should rejoice and be exceeding glad, for it is willed that our rewards will be great in heaven.

- **Our perfection:** We can be made perfect and complete in all the will of God. Christ is the author and finisher of our faith, and will someday present us faultless before the Father's presence where we will glory with exceeding joy.

Questions for Personal Meditation

Are you having problems accepting the will of God?

How do you view God's will when you are in a tough or difficult situation?

Do you find it difficult sometimes to look beyond the present circumstance, expecting the best? Why is it difficult?

Have you ever experienced a bad situation in your life that ultimately worked out for your good?

Do you know and have you truly accepted the plan God has for your life, and is it moving forward?

What excuse do you have for not following Jesus when times get hard?

A Prayer from the Heart

*Heavenly Father, we pray for thy will to be done on earth as it is in heaven. Thank you for sending your Son, Jesus, to die for us, that we may be guaranteed life throughout eternity. Fill us with the knowledge of your will in all wisdom and spiritual knowledge. Grant us the wisdom to submit to your divine will daily. Help us to realize that, as we submit to your will and study and let your Word guide our choices, that we will live lives that are truly worthy of you.
In Jesus' name we pray, Amen.*

CHAPTER 5

Time Produces Evidence of Spiritual Blessings

*But they that wait upon the Lord shall
renew their strength;
they shall mount up with wings as eagles;
they shall run, and not be weary;
and they shall walk, and not faint.*
(Isaiah 40:31)

God is our source of power and strength when we are tired of dealing with the guilt of our past, when we are worn out or weak because of the storms of life, and when our hearts are broken and filled with pain. Some, if not all of us, at one time or another, have been to the point of exhaustion where we wanted to just give up. God does not want us to give up. He will help us to endure, for he does have a purpose and plan for our lives.

Waiting on God requires waiting for divine direction in every area of our lives. Someone once said that God is not obligated to complete anything he did not start.

We have a tendency of getting in a hurry to satisfy the desires of the flesh or others. We also allow others to put us in positions for self-gratification. We are encouraged to do a good job, and we do, and receive a lot of pats on the back. But is that what God wants us to do? Are we doing this so he can be glorified?

In retrospect, during my early years in Las Vegas, I remember that I dreamed several times about walking with a group of people. I don't remember where I was going, but all of a sudden, some supernatural force took me above everyone else, "like an angel with wings."

At times in the dream, I was taken far into the clouds where I saw serenity that existed only well above the earth. Storms in our lives will come, and when we least expect it. But like an eagle, God will take us above the storms. God always has a better purpose and plan for our lives than we do. He has revealed to me that he does not want us to stay in the same old condition we are in. He wants his people, who are called by his name, to grow and "fly like an eagle." In our daily walk with God, we can make spiritual progress. He has promised us his strength, for we have none of our own.

The Bible says that when we are dead in trespasses and sins, God will quicken us and will raise us up together and will make us sit in heavenly places.

The Bible teaches us, *"If any man be in Christ, he is a new creature: old things are passed away; behold, all things are become new"* (2 Corinthians 5:17). Have you ever played the "what-if" game? Many do so as children. If we had the chance to come back as someone else or something else, who or what would it be? Well, because I loved the beauty of butterflies and peacocks, I remember I said I would want to come back as a butterfly.

But, as time passed and as I began to grow in the grace and the knowledge of our Lord and Savior Jesus Christ, I found out that my life on this earth can be similar to that of a beautiful butterfly as I go from grace to grace. First of all, a butterfly is changed from a caterpillar to a butterfly. To become saints of God, and to be born of the Spirit of God, we must be changed from the old to the new man in Christ.

Many of us were liars, thieves, fornicators, adulterers, and coveters, etc., and we were not going to inherit the kingdom of God. However, if you repent and are washed, sanctified, and justified in the name of the Lord Jesus, then by the Spirit of God, you shall inherit the kingdom. Before a caterpillar becomes a butterfly, metamorphosis takes place, where it goes from the larval stage to the pupal stage and then into the adult form. While the caterpillar is growing, it sheds its skin several times. This process of shedding old skin and growing new skin is called molting.

Before we become mature in Christ, we have to go through spiritual metamorphosis. There are some apparent attitude and behavior changes that can and must be made. We must be transformed from proud to meek, worst to best, foolish to wise, fearful to courageous, diseased to healthy, weak to strong, last to first, ruined to redeemed, drunk to sober, lying to truthful, thieving to honest, burdened to blessed, perverted to pure, immoral to moral, and hypocritical to holy. The list can go on and on.

The caterpillar struggles in its cocoon while it is being developed into a butterfly. As Christians, we go through life struggles that make us strong in the faith.

Butterflies are pollinators. They transfer pollen from one flower to another to start the process where seeds are formed.

As Christians, we are the salt of the earth and the light of the world. The beauty of the Lord will shine through us as we glow like candles. When our light illuminates others, they will see the beauty of holiness in us, and this will help them to understand the power of God working in and through us.

As we go to and fro, letting our light so shine, we may get weary, but the Scriptures tell us that we can be strengthened and renewed by the Holy Spirit. We can then claim the new name that is spoken of in Isaiah 56:5: *"Even unto them will I give in mine house and within my walls a place and a name better than of sons and of daughters: I will give them an everlasting name, that shall not be cut off."*

This is also seen in Psalm 40:3, *"And he hath put a new song in my mouth, even praise unto our God: many shall see it, and fear, and shall trust in the Lord."* Not too long ago, the Holy Spirit gave me a song, and I heard myself singing in the Spirit "Jesus, I adore you." The lyrics and the melody were in my heart. And I used this song to praise him during my meditation alone with him. I truly adore him because of his grace: the unmerited favor, mercy, and compassion he has shown toward me.

Ironically, one Sunday morning when I was to deliver a message during the 8:00 A.M. service, there was no one available to do the solo. I was then asked to sing before the sermon. The Holy Spirit allowed that time for me to share that song with the congregation:

> Jesus, I adore you.
> You have given me hope,
> You have given me joy,
> You have given me peace,
> That's why, Jesus, I adore you.
>
> Jesus, I magnify you.
> You have given me hope,
> You have given me joy,
> You have given me peace,
> That's why, Jesus, I magnify you.

Jesus, I glorify you.
You have given me hope,
You have given me joy,
You have given me peace,
That's why, Jesus, I glorify you.

Going from Grace to Grace

Time will tell the story. As I look back over my life, my journey has not always been easy, and it is certainly not complete, but my faith in the almighty God has never faltered. Our pathway to spiritual fullness is waiting on God and moving at his command, and he will take us from grace to grace.

When going from grace to grace, we must realize that first and foremost, grace is the source of our salvation. We have become a recipient of this grace and have been made alive in Christ. We are justified freely by his grace through the redemption that is in Christ Jesus. As a result, we don't have to look at ourselves the way we used to be, allowing the past guilt burden us down. Secondly, it is through grace that we have the Christian call of God to exercise the gifts he has entrusted with us. Quoting Paul in Galatians 1:15: *"But when it pleased God, who separated me from my mother's womb, and called me by his grace."*

According to the Scripture, I also declare that **God's grace is undeserved.** 1 Timothy 1:12–16 says:

> *And I thank Christ Jesus our Lord, who hath enabled me, for that he counted me faithful, putting me into the ministry; Who was before a blasphemer, and a persecutor, and injurious: but I obtained mercy, because I did it ignorantly in unbelief. And the grace of our Lord was exceeding abundant with faith and*

> *love which is in Christ Jesus. This a faithful saying, and worthy of all acceptation, that Christ Jesus came into the world to save sinners; of whom I am chief. Howbeit for this cause I obtained mercy, that in me first Jesus Christ might shew forth all longsuffering, for a pattern to them which should hereafter believe on him to life everlasting.*

God's grace is abundant, according to Romans 5:15–20. From the Living Bible paraphrased:

> *And what a difference between man's sin and God's forgiveness! For this one man, Adam, brought death to many through his sin. But this one man, Jesus Christ, brought forgiveness to many through God's mercy. Adam's one sin brought the penalty of death to many, while Christ freely takes away many sins and gives glorious life instead. The sin of this one man, Adam, caused death to be king over all, but all who will take God's gift of forgiveness and acquittal are kings of life because of this one man, Jesus Christ. Yes, Adam's sin brought punishment to all, but Christ's righteousness makes men right with God, so that they can live. Adam caused many to be sinners because he disobeyed God, and Christ caused many to be made acceptable to God because he obeyed. The Ten Commandments were given so that all could see the extent of their failure to obey God's laws. But the more we see our sinfulness, the more we see God's abounding grace forgiving us.*

Lastly, **God's grace is all-sufficient**. We read in 2 Corinthians 12:9: *"And he said unto me, My grace is sufficient for thee: for my strength is made perfect in weakness."*

As I was moved through the power of the Holy Spirit, from grace to grace, from one spiritual level to another while sharing the message of Jesus Christ to others, I thought it would be befitting that I share with you from my sermons, some of the **stepping stones** used as I moved:

Do not be ashamed of the gospel or be a shame to the gospel
Lesson from Romans 1:16

There are some so-called Christians who are a shame to the gospel. They want to hold on to God's hand and still walk with the world, dishonoring God by their wrongdoing and improper behavior. The source of the gospel is Jesus Christ. If we are not ashamed of the gospel, we are not embarrassed, afraid, or humiliated to proclaim that the gospel is the power of God unto salvation, that it saved wretches like us, and that it is far better than silver and gold.

If we are not ashamed of the gospel, we can be the chosen vessels that God wants us to be. God has all the power to do whatever, to whomever, whenever he pleases. No matter how high or how low we are, he can make a difference in our lives.

Jesus said in Mark 8:38: *"Whosoever therefore shall be ashamed of me and of my words in this adulterous and sinful generation; of him shall the Son of man be ashamed, when he cometh in the glory of his Father with the holy angels."*

We are reflections of our message
Lesson from Luke 10:16

As ministers, servants, ambassadors, or whatever our calling is, we must be all about what we teach, preach, sing, and shout about. When I was in grade school, I used to admire nurses, nutritionists, and physical education teachers in the secular world in addition to some of the leaders in the church. They were the reflections of what they taught. But, when I look at some of them today, and hear their messages on eating right, exercising, maintaining proper weight, and in the church, obeying the Word of God, their messages are separated from them.

The message of Jesus Christ that we are to proclaim to the world through our words and deeds is not only in what is said and done, but also who said it and how it is said. The method we use and our attitude toward others cannot be separated from message. We are God's channels through which he ministers to the world. We are the light of the world and the salt of the earth. It is through us that God desires to save the world, so we are under an obligation.

Have a new attitude toward the things of God
Lesson from Daniel 5:1–9

If you are stuck in the past with the same old attitudes, it will rob you of the blessings God has in store for you in the present. As it is written, "Eye hath not seen, nor ear heard, neither have entered into the heart of man, the things which God hath prepared for them that love him" (1 Corinthians 2:9). God will reveal to us by his Spirit the areas in all of our lives that need some improvement.

It's dangerous to handle holy things in a light manner. When you handle holy things in a light way, the judgment of God will show up. Marriage is honorable and was instituted by God. If we handle it the wrong way, there are some consequences. Wives, you are to submit unto your own husbands as unto the Lord. Husbands, you are to love your wives as Christ loved the church. Children are a heritage of the Lord. There is a way we correct, counsel, and caution them. Do it with wisdom from God. Our attitude of worship should be one of praise and thanksgiving. In our giving, our tenth is holy unto the Lord. If our attitude is not right for giving, we shut down the flow of blessings that God wants to rain on us.

Some of us still want to walk in the carnal mind, to walk in what we know, how we feel, or how we see things. This may work on the job, in school, or in social organizations, but not in the church. Paul said that we walk by faith and not by sight. When you try to get five out of two plus two, it will not work in the natural. In the spiritual, God can make two plus two equal one hundred.

Great things can happen when we believe
Lesson from Matthew 21:22

Our entire Christian life should be governed by faith and prayer. This will enable us to overcome obstacles that are like mountains that would hinder our service to God. We must ask the Holy Spirit to lead us to ask for the right things—and when he does this, he will also give us the faith to believe. We need faith to believe. Faith is the action word; it includes trust in the unseen reality. When it comes to receiving anything from the Lord, someone once said, "It is like water, and will do you no good unless you use it."

All of us have a bitter cup to drink from in this life. The quantity of sufferings, disappointments, heartaches, trials, and worries in our cups varies. Some are compelled to drink a few drops of it, while others are required to drink from the cup that is filled to the brim. No matter how bitter the cup is and how much we drink from it, we can always find relief and comfort in knowing that God hears and answers our prayers, and that he is still in control.

Together in unity
Lesson from 1 Corinthians 1:10

When we come together in unity, in agreement, all of us

will come to the table with something to offer. God has blessed us with an abundance of spiritual gifts in the church. We need to use what we have, and we should not want for anything. If we commit our ways to God, he promised to provide all our needs.

We should all agree on the basic teachings of our faith. We should not be separated into different groups in the church that tend to promote rivalry and competition. We should not lift anyone else above Christ, for he is the head. We should work toward the same goal and settle all matters that may keep us divided. Our minds should be open toward each other, showing kindness, love, and respect.

When we come together, our motives should be the same—to worship and to serve God—even if we don't agree on how to do it. It is the love of God that will create togetherness. The love of God will destroy selfishness, solve our problems, improve our relationships, and heal our conflicts.

Women should labor together with God
Lesson from 1 Corinthians 3:9

Without discrimination, all persons, male and female, have the honor and responsibility to proclaim the good news of Jesus Christ. God has no respect of persons. He can use anyone who has a willing heart, a dedicated life, and a prayer to be filled with Holy Spirit.

Spirit-directed women also need to have a proper balance of activities in our lives. It is possible that we can get so caught up in the service for the Lord that we neglect those things such as family and home. If we are so busy that we cannot pay attention to our husbands or listen attentively to our children and or grandchildren, we will not be able to do an effective work for the Lord. On the other hand, don't use your home and family as excuses for not getting involved.

We experience joy in knowing that we are never alone,

and that our labor is not in vain, in spite of the adversities we may experience in our laboring. There is joy in spite of hardships, discouragements, frustrations, and perplexities. Psalm 30:5 says, *"Weeping may endure for a night, but joy cometh in the morning."* This is real joy, unspeakable joy, unbelievable joy, and undeniable joy.

Don't be worried if you should miss out here on earth on receiving rewards for your faithfulness, recognition of your accomplishments, acknowledgments of your abilities, praises for your leadership, credit for your sacrificial giving, and proper respect for your ministry. It is all because of Christ, and heaven will more than make up for it.

Be ready
Lesson from Matthew 25:1–13

We must prepare ourselves for the second coming of Christ. Paul said in 1 Thessalonians 4:16–17: *"For the Lord himself shall descend from heaven with a shout, with the voice of the archangel, and with the trump of God: and the dead in Christ shall rise first: Then we which are alive and remain shall be caught up together with them in the clouds, to meet the Lord in the air: and so shall we ever be with the Lord."*

God's desire is not for us to cram for the finals, because time wasted can be regretted later. If we study for the finals day by day, we can grow into the likeness of God's Son and be ready when he comes back for us.

When we develop the kind of love that Christ had for us, and the devotion he had to do the will of his Father, we will always be ready for his return. No one knows God's timetable. It would be foolish for us to stay in this world with little or no preparation, until the last minute, and then try to play hopscotch and try to skip into the kingdom.

A poem written by Roy Lessin truly has been an encouragement to me:

In His Time

I wait on God to bring
to pass all he has promised me,
and as I wait,
I will rest in faith in what I cannot see,
for in his way he will provide
at just the right time,
everything that's good and right,
to bless this life of mine.

Questions for Personal Meditation

Does your spiritual closet need a spring cleaning?

Are you still having a struggle between obeying the flesh and yielding to the Spirit in a certain area of your life?

What is the reason for this struggle?

Are there any areas of your life you need to surrender to God?

What can you do to experience God's control in your life?

Why is it difficult sometimes to wait on God?

Can you relate recent evidence of God's grace in your life?

A Prayer from the Heart

Thank you, Lord, for the multitude of spiritual blessings you have bestowed upon us. We thank you for your grace that is freely given and that is sufficient for all our needs. Encourage our hearts to wait on you, realizing that your grace that is given to us will empower us as we submit according to your will. We magnify, glorify, adore, and appreciate you, in Jesus' name, Amen.

CHAPTER 6

God's Glory Is Revealed in Every Situation

*But we all, with open face beholding as in a glass
the glory of the Lord, are changed into the same
image from glory to glory, even as the Spirit of the Lord.*
(2 Corinthians 3:18)

Many years ago we went through some changes in our church regarding leadership. Sometime later, one of the members came to me and said, "I was watching your demeanor all through the horrific ordeal, and you seemed to have an inner peace." During those trying times, some unpleasant comments were made regarding my family that some made sure that I heard. The hurt was there, but in time, it went away like sand in the wind, for my God erased it all.

The members at that time were looking at a small part of the whole picture. But, we should not be dismayed at what we see at the moment, for according to God's plan, there is a bigger and better picture.

The Word of God is like a mirror, and when we go through our storms of life, we can see God's glory revealed.

We don't have to wait until Christ's return to experience his glory. Every day we can be in his presence from glory to glory as we grow to become more like him.

Even when we go through difficult times, we must take off our masks of deception and let God work through us, so that others might see what God is doing in us. We must reflect the Lord's glory as we are transformed into his likeness through the adversities.

In chapter 11 of the book of John, we read the story of Christ raising Lazarus to life, which is a witness to the glory of God. In verse 4, after Jesus heard that Lazarus was sick, he said, *"This sickness is not unto death, but for the glory of God, that the Son of God might be glorified thereby."* After Lazarus died, Jesus went to the grave where Lazarus was laid, and said to Martha, Lazarus's sister, in verse 40: *"Said I not unto thee, that, if thou wouldest believe, thou shouldest see the glory of God?"* When the stone was removed from the grave, he looked toward heaven and prayed. Afterwards, Jesus cried out with a loud voice to Lazarus to come forth. Death was then conquered, and many of the Jews believed in him. These Jews had come to the other sister, Mary, and had seen the things that Jesus had done.

Isaiah 40:5 tell us, *"And the glory of the Lord shall be revealed, and all flesh shall see it together: for the mouth of the Lord hath spoken it."* God's glory can be witnessed by all who come in contact with saving power and have yielded to him. His glory can also be revealed to the lost world.

In the Old Testament, the glory of God was manifested to Moses when he was called to the mountain to receive further instructions. For six days the mountain was covered by a cloud, which was a token of God's special presence there. When God called Moses out of the midst of the cloud, the thick cloud opened in the sight of all Israel, and the glory of the Lord broke forth with devouring fire. Moses went into the midst of the fire knowing that God would

God's Glory Is Revealed in Every Situation

protect him.

In the New Testament, Acts chapter 7, the glory of God was manifested to Stephen. Israel had crucified Christ and allowed John the Baptist to be slain. Now, when Stephen was about to be slain, he lifted up his eyes to heaven and saw the glory of God and Christ standing on the right hand of his Father.

The glory of God was revealed in Christ: even while he was hanging on the cross, he prayed for his enemies (Luke 23:34). He welcomed the thief with the promise of paradise in Luke 23:43, and he still welcomes us back with open arms today. He is also the author and finisher of our faith and sits on the right hand of the throne of God where he is still interceding for us

Isaiah 43:1–2 tells us what God will do for him to be glorified. The Living Bible paraphrase words it as follows: *"But now the Lord who created you, O Israel, says, Don't be afraid, for I have ransomed you; I have called you by name; you are mine. When you go through deep waters and great trouble, I will be with you. When you go through rivers of difficulty, you will not drown! When you walk through the fire of oppression, you will not be burned up—the flames will not consume you."*

Adversities in our lives will come for many reasons:

- Reason number 1: to humble us. 2 Chronicles 33:12: *"And when he was in affliction, he besought the Lord his God, and humbled himself greatly before the God of his fathers."*

- Reason number 2: to chastise and correct us. Hebrews 12:6–7: *"For whom the Lord loveth he chasteneth, and scourgeth every son whom he receiveth. If ye endure chastening, God dealeth with you as with sons; for what son is he whom the father chasteneth not?"*

- Reason number 3: to test our faith. 1 Peter 1:5–8: *"Who are kept by the power of God through faith unto salvation ready to be revealed in the last time. Wherein ye greatly rejoice, though now for a season, if need be, ye are heaviness through manifold temptations: That the trial of your faith, being much more precious than of gold that perisheth, though it be tried with fire, might be found unto praise and honour and glory at the appearing of Jesus Christ: Whom having not seen, ye love; in whom, though now ye see him not, yet believing, ye rejoice with joy unspeakable and full of glory."*

- Reason number 4: to give us final rest. Psalm 94:13: *"That thou mayest give him rest from the days of adversity, until the pit be digged for the wicked."*

Survival Through Adversities

We can survive through all of our adversities, if we look for the glory in our trials. The Bible teaches us that God's glory is far greater than our present sufferings, for our present sufferings are not worthy to be compared. Not only do we have hope for the future because of our sufferings, but we can also have daily confidence in the present trials of life.

A few months before our daughter was to graduate from college, we received another frantic call from her. She was told by one of the officials of the university that she may not be allowed to graduate until the following year. As the story was told, one of her classmates had been injured after a fraternity party by one of her suitemates. This person withdrew from school a few days after the incident, and our daughter was identified to take the fall because of the way the incident started during the party.

After she had attended several meetings at the university about the situation, we were advised to get an attorney because the parents of the injured party were very influential with the university. After much prayer, my husband decided to go to Louisiana and face the accusers. To our disappointment, every attorney he contacted, even a friend of one our family members, did not want to touch the case because of their ties to the university.

Since we believe in God's Word and the power of prayer, I looked beyond the situation and petitioned the almighty God again. The next person that the Holy Spirit led us to took on the university on our behalf.

No matter how dark things seem to be, no matter what men might say, I am convinced that God is still in control and is looking after the welfare of his people. I am also convinced that, if God be for us, who can be against us? Our daughter did not march in the graduation ceremonies, but she attended and received her BA degree in Clinical Psychology.

Questions for Personal Meditation

How much does your life reflect characteristics of a worldly Christian? A spiritual Christian?

Do you want people to see what Christ is doing in your life? Or do you want them to see how good you are?

How can you experience victory in your life?

How can one see Jesus in your life?

Are you honest in sharing your personal weaknesses and needs?

A Prayer from the Heart

We praise you, Father, for your peace that surpasseth all understanding and keeps our hearts and minds. Even though we may not fully understand certain situations that unfold before our eyes, we believe that you are still in control. Continue to give us a sense of peace through all of our adversities, and a hope that will take us through eternity. Help us continually to recognize that in all things you are to be glorified, through your Son, Jesus Christ. For it is in his name that we pray, Amen

CHAPTER 7

The End of Life Is Just a Puff Away

*Whereas ye know not what be on the morrow.
For what is your life? It is even a vapour,
that appeareth for a little time,
and then vanisheth away.*
(James 4:14)

I remember as a college student trying to fit in with the crowd by developing a habit for smoking menthol cigarettes. I never mastered that vice. I would inhale, almost choking, and then as a comforting relief, exhale. As I exhaled the smoke, I noticed that it would vanish into the air like vapor. I soon realized that if I continued this habit, it would leave a damaging effect on the inside, and the Holy Spirit will not dwell therein.

Our life is described as a vapor in the book of James. The length of our life is uncertain as the morning fog – now you see it; then you don't. The shortness of our life is also described in various ways throughout the Bible:

- As a pilgrimage—Genesis 47:9
- As a shadow—1 Chronicles 29:15
- As a cloud—Job 7:9
- As a flower—Job 14:1–2
- As a dream—Job 20:8
- As sleep—Psalm 90:
- As a tale told—Psalm 90:9
- As grass—1 Peter 1:24

I've heard it said that someone died an untimely death. According to the Word of God, there is a time and season for everything under the sun. There is a time to be born and a time to die. When we have finished the work that has been laid out for us before the beginning of time, we have to make an exit and enter into eternity.

So then, what should our attitude toward life be? Psalm 90:12 says, *"So teach us to number our days, that we may apply our hearts unto wisdom."* And in Colossians 4:5 we read, *"Walk in wisdom toward them that are without, redeeming the time."*

We must realize the brevity of life and let our living be serious according to Ephesians 5:15: *"See that we walk circumspectly, not as fools, but as wise."*

We waste a lot of time, energy, money, talents in what is apart from God's will, and we may never recover the lost opportunity. We must make the most of every opportunity for doing good. Take the time each day to touch somebody's life in a positive way so that God might be glorified.

I have observed over the years how some get in a hurry, once a week, and come to the house of worship, usually on Sunday, dressed in their finest clothes, to show others how God has materially blessed them. In addition, they:

- Show up
- Show off

- Show out

The Bible does teach us to forsake not the assembling of ourselves together. However, sometimes the assembling together is for the wrong reasons. Since our time is limited, we must have concern and include time for others. There is no time for self-centered living, especially in the church.

I have also noticed that some come together sometimes with their gearshift in the "I Mode":

I have heard it said that, these are worldly Christians who have allowed Christ to enter their life, but are still being controlled by the desires of the flesh.
- I just got a fat promotion
- I've got the largest house on the block
- I've got two big cars in my garage so I have to park the third one on the street
- I am going on a cruise next week

We are not too concerned with:

- The young mother sitting next to you who has just lost her job and has no other means of supporting her family.

- The deacon whose son did not come home last night from a drug outing, which caused him to lose some sleep, and is the main reason he can hardly stay awake during service.

- The mother on the usher board, who is having difficulty paying bills because her unsaved husband is not taking care of his responsibility.

- The new convert who is still struggling with a weight or sin, and is not sure of her salvation.

- The once faithful member who is now at home due to illness and has not been seen in months.

- The elderly gentleman who is not participating like he used to because it is all about youth.

- The wife who is trying to follow the Word of God but is having a hard time dealing with the command to "submit yourself to your own husband" because of verbal or physical abuse.

We must live so someone else can live, because the end of all things is at hand. We must live in anticipation, and in expectation, of the coming of our Lord and Savior Jesus Christ. Our eyes must stay focused on him as we wait for the second coming. Time is winding up. Come out of your comfort zone and reach out in love. God desperately needs people to make a positive impact within the church, community, state, and nation by representing God's kingdom on earth, based on God's will and his Word.

What happens to our fellow church members should be important to us because we are many members, but one body in Christ. If one member of the body is hurting, is experiencing difficulties or tragedies, or is struggling with a weakness, the entire body will suffer.

The members of the body must care for each other so together we will mature in Christ. We are to help encourage and restore each other to a useful life in Christ.

In April of 1997, I participated in a regional conference workshop held in Salt Lake City, Utah, where I shared on the topic, "The Eyes of the Righteous Are Focused on God as They Wait for the Second Coming." I pointed out that a long time has passed since Christ gave his pledge to return. No matter how many centuries have come and gone, however, the one who conquered death must be taken seri-

The End of Life Is Just a Puff Away

ously—both as to his promise and the warnings he uttered—lest his return take us by surprise and find us uninterested and unprepared.

God will come suddenly and unexpectedly, as a thief in the night. Each day that we mark off the calendar brings us closer to the coming of the Lord. With God a day may be as a thousand years, and a thousand years as a day. Perhaps it will be today, tomorrow, next month, next year, or the next century. It will happen, and it will happen according to God's predetermined plan. In the light of his promise and the fact that life is just a puff away, we must continue to focus on God. We must wait for him to say our time is up on this earth, we have finished the work he had assigned for us to do, and we have to move on to a better place that he has prepared for the righteous.

We must set a good example. Whether we want to be are not, we are setting an example of some kind (good or bad). Somebody wants to pattern his or her life after you and me. As Christians, we are marked because we are children of God and people are watching to see what children of God are like. How do we react under pressure? What do we do when the going gets tough? What do we do when there seems to be no way out? At work, at school, in our neighborhood, and even in the church, people have problems and they want answers for them. Christ promises us an answer to every life situation. So, if we are in Christ, they want to see if it works.

We must live one day at a time, and we must do according to the Word of God. Our adversaries are also watching and seeking an occasion to find something wrong to pick holes in our teaching and behavior.

God is our only designer of the pattern we are to follow in setting a good example in our Christian walk. There are no separate instructions for the young, old, rich, poor, black, white, yellow, Jew, or Gentile. One size fits all—everybody must follow the same instructions.

I love to sew, especially by patterns. The guide sheets in the commercial patterns give directions on how to lay out, cut, and put together the pieces, usually by sections. I constantly recheck the guide sheet to make sure the item is being put together correctly, especially if it is a very difficult project, or I have never made that item before. I try not to guess at what I am doing.

The Word of God is our instruction manual for setting a good example, and the Holy Spirit enables the Word to become alive in us. We should constantly recheck (study the Word of God) to be sure we stay on track. In this world, we should take nothing for granted. Jesus tells us in Matthew 22:29: *"Ye do err, not knowing the scriptures, nor the power of God."*

I learned that the adversary is watching our words, the things we say to one another and how we say them. When I was a child growing up, when we got angry with one another, we would say, "Sticks and stones may break my bones, but words will never hurt." That was so far from the truth. Words can hurt and can also heal. The Bible says in Colossians 4:6, *"Let your speech be alway with grace, seasoned with salt, that ye may know how ye ought to answer every man."*

Do All the Good You Can While You Can

When Donald Ray, one of my younger brothers, passed away in 1998, it was devastating. I did not realize he was sick enough to die sooner than later. I had received a letter from him saying that he was ill and that he would tell me about his illness later. The day before he passed away, I called to speak with him and was told that he was asleep.

The thought that I did not get a chance to talk with him about some important issues haunted me for a long time.

We can become so preoccupied with ourselves that we

The End of Life Is Just a Puff Away

sometimes tune out the needs of others. We must realize that the lives we live are not unto ourselves, for we were bought with a price. We must take the time to listen with our hearts and our spiritual ears to our family members, friends, and others we come in contact with daily so that we have no regrets.

During his home-going service, As I spoke words of encouragement to the family, I read excerpts from a poem he had written and sent to me a year earlier. After reading his poem below over and over again, I was finally given the confirmation that he was ready to go home to be with the Lord, and my fear had subsided:

Our Father

Our Father will tell us no lie,
because it is said we
will never die.

We walk around all day long,
but we don't know
when he may call us home.

Sometimes we're up and
sometimes we're down.
They got some humans think they can't
go underground.

We bow down and say
our prayers, we even got
some who would swear.

We walk around all day long,
but we don't even know
when we were born.

For His Name's Sake

He don't just love them,
He wants all his children
to be with him.

So listen my children; and
don't you fear, because our
Father is very near.

He gave us a mother
and he gave us a father,
He even gave us a loving brother.

He created the heavens, and
He created the sun. He loved
us so much, he sent his only Son.

Our Father's Son that he loves
so dear, we got some people who
don't know he is very near.

The mother that little brother
was born in, she was so good,
that she had no sin.

They had some people who
did him so bad, but what they
done to him made a lot of people mad.

They have some people talk about
our brother both day and night.
They got some said he was wrong,
and some said he was right. But
they don't know he will never be
out of their sight.

The End of Life Is Just a Puff Away

Listen my children and
don't you cry, because we have
a Father who will tell you no lie.

We got some people who
try to be bad, but they don't
know who will take them
and make them sad.

Listen my children and
listen well, we have a Father
who don't want you to go to hell.

He will be with us
day and night, he don't
want us out of his sight.

We walk around all day long,
but we don't know
when he will call us home.

Father! Father! Please look
over my cry, I just want
to be with you in the sky.

*Donald Ray Williams
"Monk"*

 It matters not how long we live, but rather what we do while we live. Jesus' ministry on earth lasted only three and one-half years, and yet he completed all the things necessary to accomplish his father's purpose for him. In Ecclesiastes 3:1, we learn that "There is an appointed time for every-thing—-A time to do every thing God wants us to do". Our purpose for spiritual life is found in 1 Thessalonians 5:9–11:

"For God hath not appointed us to wrath, but to obtain salvation by our Lord Jesus Christ, Who died for us, that, whether we wake or sleep, we should live together with him. Wherefore comfort yourselves together, and edify one another, even as also ye do."

To accomplish our purpose in life, I would like to offer the following steps. First, we must make a choice to serve God. *"I call heaven and earth to record this day against you, that I have set before you life and death, blessing and cursing: therefore choose life, that both thou and thy seed may live"* (Deuteronomy 30:19).

Second, we must seek God's kingdom. *"But seek ye first the kingdom of God, and his righteousness; and all these things shall be added unto you"* (Matthew 6:33). *"For every one that asketh receiveth; and he that seeketh findeth; and to him that knocketh it shall be opened"* (Luke 11:10).

Third, we must be submissive to the divine will of our father who art in heaven. *"I delight to do thy will, O my God: yea, the law is within my heart"* (Psalm 40:8).

Fourth, we must seek Christ likeness. *"Brethren, I count not myself to have apprehended: but this one thing I do, forgetting those things which are behind, and reaching forth unto those things which are before, I press toward the mark for the prize of the high calling of God in Christ Jesus"* (Philippians 3:13–14).

Fifth, we must finish the divine task. *"I have glorified thee on the earth: I have finished the work which thou gavest me to do"* (John 17:4).

Finally, we must complete our task joyfully. *"But none of these things move me, neither count I my life dear unto myself, so that I might finish my course with joy, and the ministry, which I have received of the Lord Jesus, to testify the gospel of the grace of God"* (Acts 20:24).

We must do all the good we can while we can. We must work the work of Christ who sent us, for when night comes, none of us will be able to work. At the end of day it is time for self-evaluation. This is taken from an anonymous writing:

> Is anyone happier I passed this way?
> Does anybody remember that I spoke to him today?
> The day is almost over, and toiling time is through.
> Is there anyone to utter now a kindly word of me?"
>
> Can I say tonight in parting with the day that's slipping fast,
> That I helped a single brother of the many that I passed?
> Is a single heart rejoicing over what I did or said?
> Does the man whose hopes were fading now with courage look ahead?
>
> Did I waste the day or lose it, was it well or poorly spent?
> Did I leave a trail of kindness or a scar of discontent?
> As we close our eyes in slumber do you think that God will say,
> "You have earned one more tomorrow by the work you did today"?

Questions for Personal Meditation

Would God be pleased with how you spend your time daily? Would you consider making a change? Why is the wise use of your time today so important?

How much time do you spend in the word of God?

How is your current relationship with members of your family? Church?

Do you want to improve the relationships? How?

Have you recently been an encouragement to someone in his or her hour of despair?

Did you actually enter into his or her life and stay with it?

Do you seek reconciliation with those you have a problem with?

A Prayer from the Heart

God, our creator and sustainer, we are grateful for the breath of life, realizing that our life is in your hands. Help us to be ever mindful of the importance of our time here on this earth, so that we may make good use of it daily. We do not know the day or the hour when you will come for us. Grant us wisdom and patience to be good listeners, especially when dealing with family members. Continue to give us a vision regarding the needs of others and how we can help. We ask it all in Jesus' name, Amen.

APPENDIX

Unforgettable Moments

As a first-time mom, the excitement of seeing our first child mature from one stage to another is inevitable: turning over for the first time, saying the first word, cutting the first tooth, etc.

We also looked forward with great anticipation to the first step being taken, and we remember how we ran to protect the child from the fall. When the cord is finally broken, and the child is off to preschool for the first time, we remember the cry when the goodbye was said, and how a stranger would be watching your flower bloom during the sunlight.

As a first-time grandmother, there is also anticipation and moments of triumph with great joy that we can testify to. Etched in my memory is the morning of May 4, 1989, at Women's Hospital when a nurse met me in the hallway with a beautiful six-pound, seven-ounce baby girl, and said, "Congratulations, Grandmother." I had just finished signing my daughter in and was on my way to her room. I was then told by the nurse to follow her, and to my amazement, I was given the opportunity to bathe my granddaughter.

When I recall the incident, I can still picture in my mind the tub with the warm, sudsy water and the feel of it as I washed her.

When Ja'nel was a preschooler, one Saturday morning as we were on our way to buy groceries, I began to share with her some things her mother and I used to do on the weekends. With curious eyes, she looked at me and said, "Where was I, Grandma?" I immediately responded, "Why, you were in heaven with Jesus." To my amazement, she replied, "I remember that because God told me you were going to be my grandmother." How could you forget this incident? You just can't.

Parents are overwhelmed with joy and delight upon the birth of their children. Our hearts should rejoice when there is a spiritual new birth for our children and grandchildren.

I remember the day when Ja'nel came forth. When she was almost five, she made a commitment and accepted Christ as her Savior, and was baptized. This memorable moment put tears in my eyes and caused my heart to rejoice, knowing that she had made the most important decision of her life. Her mind has always been more mature than those of her age group.

During the time Ja'nel that attended the elementary magnet school, she had to do a photo essay on her personal hero. I was blessed to be the one chosen by her. She wrote, and I quote: "I chose her because she cares about me, loves me, and is a great Christian mentor and friend, and of course, a great grandma." That memory was carved in stone and will never be erased.

One day in middle school, while she was on her way to lunch with two of her classmates, She shared with them what she had read from one of the books in the best-selling series entitled *Left Behind* by Jerry B. Jenkins and Tim La Haye.

She was questioned by the one who was an atheist regarding her beliefs in the rapture and tribulation period. Her quick response was that one day they may be walking together, when suddenly he will look around for her, but her cheerleader outfit will be on the ground and she will be nowhere in sight.

He then wanted to know if she was going to that place she called heaven with no clothes on.

Her astounding remark was "Yes, I came into this world with no clothes on, and I can go out with none."

I have told this anecdote several times with humor, but more importantly, with a thankful heart that her faith in the living God had deepened.

I will always remember the smiles of the other granddaughters and the way they would look at me and say, "We love you, Grandma. Can we come over to your house?" It would just melt my heart!

I decided to take a random survey of other grandmothers to share some unforgettable and memorable moments with their grandchildren. According to Proverbs 17:6, grandchildren are a crown of old men. This crown represents an emblem of splendor and honor. Grandparents are unique individuals created by God to share their wisdom and knowledge, to be sounding boards, to bridge a gap, and most of all, to be and do whatever God has willed in his sovereign plan in the lives of their grandchildren. Following are some examples in their own words.

* * *

One memorable experience I had with Donvoana at age twenty months was when he called me GiGi and tried to tell me what his mom and dad had done to him. I remember when he was eighteen months old and I first saw him try to write with a pencil. He would sit on the floor with a pencil and paper and try to write and repeat the letters as they were called out to him.

I remember when my other grandchild, Javier, at age ten months, took his first step one morning just after his father had dropped him off. He stood up by the coffee table, turned loose, took three steps forward, and then fell down and started laughing.

Regina Cone

* * *

After my granddaughter, De Andria Blankes, started her new job as a front desk clerk, she told me she was having a hard time. The people were getting on her nerves because they were very rude and they hurt her feelings. I told her, "Dee, Each morning when you get up, pray and ask God to help you with the people and to understand them." She told me, "I do pray." I then told her to keep praying, and pray all through the day.

Sammye Blankes

* * *

Thanks be unto God that I am a grandmother. When one of my granddaughters was in the tenth grade, at the end of the nine-week period, she came home and showed us her report card. I questioned her regarding her grades, because I thought they were not what they should have been. She replied that the lessons were too hard. I have always told my children and grandchildren to put God first, to pray, and to ask God to help them with their classes. To my amazement, after the next nine weeks, she came home with her card and it had three A's, three B's, and one C. I asked her again what happened, and she said, "I did what you told me to do. I will always put God first." By doing this, she is one of the top students in her class, going into her junior year.

Martha Banks

* * *

K'rell, my six-year-old grandson, calls me Grandma. One day he and I were in the kitchen and he was repeatedly calling me: "Grandma! Grandma!" So I stopped him and said, "I am not your grandma but your grandmother." He then waited a little while and started to call me Grandma again, but then caught himself and said, "Grandmmmmmm," and then looked at me and said, "I don't have time to say all of that grandmother or whatever."

One day we were all going to the store. Dewanda, who is K'rell's mother, was talking and said "breast chicken." K'rell looked at her and said, "Da."

I will always remember the spiritual moments I share with K'rell. He loves to sing spiritual hymns in the car when we are on our way to church and when we are together delivering pies. He loves to sing, "This little light of mine, I'm going to let it shine," and he also adds into it, "I woke up this morning with my mind still on Jesus, and I am going to let it shine."

K'rell was baptized on Sunday, November 3, 2002. A few days before he was to be baptized, I was talking with him about how the pastor would baptize him and how he was going to be taken under the water. He replied, "I'm not scared of anything, Grandma!"

K'wan, my youngest grandson at two years old, is very observant. I make pies and he wants to know what all goes into them. When he is in the kitchen with me, he sometimes wants to add more than necessary, so I have to watch him very closely.

Irma Craft

* * *

There is something memorable about each day that I spend with my grandson. But, the first most memorable experience was spending thirty-six hours in the birthing center with his mother and then sitting behind the doctor watching him being born. I had the opportunity to hold him before his mother or father and even before the nurse gave him his bath. The second most memorable experience was seeing him take his first step and start to walk.

He had just turned one year old, and I had taken him to Monroe, Louisiana, so his ninety-one-year-old great-great-uncle could see him. I had told his mom, "When I get back, he will be walking." Well, when we got back to Phoenix, Arizona, he wasn't walking. Later on that night, I stood him up and said to him, "Walk to Mommy." She held out her hand and he took his first step. He wouldn't walk back to me, but he would walk to his mom. He has been moving ever since (with too much energy).

Beatrice Randle

* * *

From a child's point of view, the grandparents' home is also available and a safe haven. When my daughter and her husband were discussing with their two sons the possibility of losing their new house, if they went to Disneyland instead of paying the mortgage, the youngest son replied "Well, let's go to Disneyland because we can go and stay at our grandmother's house."

Lula Williams

* * *

It is an honor for me to share with the readers a few

Unforgettable Moments

memorable moments with my grandson, Christopher Clary. The first is his birth. Words cannot express the joy when the doctor took Chris from his mother and placed him into my arms. The nurse allowed me to take him in to be cleaned, and he never left my eyes from the time he came down the birth canal until they had weighed, measured, and footprinted him. I had them put those little footprints all over the back of my gown, and he still has my permission to walk on my back.

I remember when he was about three years old, we would be riding and I would give him a letter and a color for the day. He would get so excited when he would see the color or the letter of the alphabet on something, because he looked forward to showing me that he knew the color or letter.

When Chris started school, I was wearing a double upright leg brace. We know how cruel little children can appear to be. Well, I took Chris to school every day, and on occasion, I would stay and be the room mom. On one occasion, one of his little classmates would make a remark about my disability and little Chris said, "It is OK that her leg is not good; my grandmother comes to school with me. Where is your grandmother?"

Shirley Davis

* * *

This was an exciting experience, but I have to say it was also a happy one. Sometimes we expect things in life to come biologically, but that may not always be so. God's plan for our lives is not always what we expect. I have a sweet little grandchild, Gieyonny Clark, born August 2, 1999. When I came home from church the evening before, I noticed a diaper bag packed on the table. Around 10:30 P.M. that night, I asked her mother what was it packed for, and she said she was ready to go to the hospital. Very excited, I jumped into the car and took her to the hospital. When the baby was born, I was sitting in the corner of the room praying that the baby would be fine.

My hands were the first to hold her. To be honest, I was afraid to hold her because she was so little. She is now three years old and very knowledgeable. We read together and pray together. Being a grandmother is a privilege. I am so blessed to have this little grandchild, for she reminds me of things important that I sometimes forget. Oh, yes, she can get in my way a lot of times, but the little bundle of joy makes up for it all. My prayer is that she will grow to be a vessel for the Master's use. There is never a dull moment when Gieyonny's around. I thank God for her.

Estella Kline

* * *

I am the happy grandmother of nine. One day one of my grandchildren by the name of Alecia and I were on our way to the market, and I began to talk aloud to God while I was driving. I did not think she was paying attention when suddenly she asked, "Granny, who are you talking to?" I said, "God." She then replied, "Where is he? I don't see him." I began to explain that you can't see him, for he is invisible. Then she wanted to know where he lived. I told her that he is everywhere: in the sky, on earth, and in the sea. Sitting next to the open window, she leaned her little body out as far as she could without falling out, looking for God in the sky. She finally said, "Well! I don't understand, Grannie. You never lie to me so it must be true, but I just don't understand." When we got home, I explained to her in the Word of God how she will come to understand.

Marrie Pullens

Reflections…

For His Name's Sake

Reflections...

Reflections...

Reflections...

Reflections…

For His Name's Sake

Reflections…

Reflections…

Epilogue

Don't say you are not important,
It's simply isn't true,
The fact that you were born,
Is proof, God has a plan for you.

The path may seen unclear right now,
But one day you will see,
That all that came before,
Was truly meant to be.

God wrote the book that is your life,
That's all you need to know.
Each day that you are living,
Was written long ago.

God only writes best sellers,
So be proud of who you are,
Your character is important,
In this book you are the "star."

Enjoy the novel as it reads,
It will stand throughout the ages,
Savor each chapter as you go,
Taking time to turn the pages.

Anon.

Printed in the United States
1031400003B